FREE LANCE and the DRAGON'S HOARD

PAUL STEWART

CHRIS RIDDELL

Barrington Stoke

1

"Wake up, Sir Knight! Wake *up*!" My eyes snapped open and I jumped to my feet. I drew my sword, ready for action.

The merchant was standing there. His eyes glinted with terror in the firelight. "It's out there!" he cried. "It's out there!"

"*What's* out there?" I asked. I put my hand on his arm to steady him.

The merchant drew his face close to mine. His skin was wet with sweat, his eyes were wide, his voice was little more than a whisper.

"The dragon, of course," he croaked.

*

I was offered this job three weeks ago. Back then, I thought that being a bodyguard to a rich merchant would be a nice little earner for a knight down on his luck. I should have known it wasn't going to be that simple. It never is.

After all, I'm a free lance, a knight for hire. Trouble always finds me, no matter where I go. Just like now.

I was broke. Skint as a juggler's monkey. Not a penny left. And what was worse, I'd lost my squire, Wormrick.

I'd had to leave him looking after his broken leg beside a blazing fire in a fine inn. He had the last of my gold coins in his pocket.

It was the least I could do after our last little adventure.

That one started with yours truly – that's me – doing a favour for a pretty duchess. I'd agreed to get a solid-gold goblet back for her. It had been "borrowed" by her wicked mother-in-law. The adventure had ended with Wormrick being chased up a set of spiral stairs by a pack of castle dogs – and then falling from the top of the tall tower.

But that's another story ...

So, I'll start with this one.

There I was, in a dusty market in a city down south. I had no squire, no money, and I needed a job – any job. But then, so did all the other knights down on their luck who had turned up in the market square that day.

I was just about to give up and go back to the town stable where I'd left Jed, my pure-bred Arbuthnot grey, when I spotted the merchant. He was tall, with a neat, clipped beard and fine clothes – silk robes, a purple turban, satin slippers. You know the type. As plump and flashy as a stuffed peacock.

The merchant had rejected ten other knights or more before he got to me, which wasn't a surprise at all.

They all looked even more down-at-heel than me. Some had cuts and bruises from old tournaments. And, from the look of their rusty armour and even more rusty swordplay, I could tell that some hadn't been in a tournament for years.

When it came to my turn, the Stuffed Peacock looked down at the sword at my side.

"Can you use that thing?" he asked.

I drew the sword in a flash and – with a flick of my hand – cut the top off the feather in his turban. He gawped at me, a look of astonishment on his face.

"Impressive," he said, as I put my sword away. "You're hired."

It turned out that he was a rich merchant. He had a dozen mules loaded up with rolls of fine silks, jars of expensive oils and sacks of fragrant spices, and he needed to get them safely from the city market to his home town. That's where I came in.

"There are many dangers along the way," he said, his voice hushed, his eyes narrow. "Robbers. Wolves. And maybe worse ..."

"I can handle most things ..." I told him, trying hard to sound cool ... "For the right price," I added.

I needed this job and this merchant looked as if he could pay well.

The Peacock didn't bat an eyelid. "Fifty gold coins if you get me and my goods to my home town safely," he said.

It was a good offer, and I didn't stop to think. That's the problem. I never do.

"Done!" I said before the Peacock could change his mind.

*

We set off nice and early the next morning. And as the sun rose, the low mist gave way to a bright, cloudless sky. The land grew dry and more empty. Large birds with curved beaks and ragged wings flew across the sky as we left the city far behind us.

It soon became clear that the merchant was right about the road we had to take. There *were* robbers – though they were easy to spot. They hung around at crossroads and in the hills above mountain passes. Robbers are easy to avoid if you check ahead and keep your eyes peeled. You need to travel in the daytime and set up a safe camp at night. The same goes for wolves, but you also need a good, bright campfire to keep them away.

Of course, with a dozen mules loaded with goods behind us and the Peacock on his jumpy white horse in front, Jed and I couldn't relax for a moment. Back and forwards we went, time after time, to make sure they were all still safe. It made us both very tired. But then again, we'd killed horrible hags and survived blood-soaked tournaments – compared to that, it was easy being a rich merchant's bodyguard.

A fortnight later, we rode up to the merchant's home town. I could almost feel those fifty gold coins jangling in my pocket.

The sun had just slipped down below the horizon when I called a halt. Peacock wasn't happy. He wanted to press on into the night and get back home, which I could understand.

But it was also foolish. Wolves like nothing better than a night hunt, and we were in classic wolf country – a flat, rocky plain, with jagged mountains all around.

There was a chill wind, which stirred up the dust and whistled between the rocks. It was spooky, but I was far too busy to let it bother me.

I had the mules to secure, Jed to settle, a fire to make, the torches to light, a meal to prepare ... As ever, the Peacock said little and did even less.

Even so, I could tell he wasn't happy. In fact, he looked as nervy as a goose in a kitchen. He flapped about as he tied his jumpy mare, Sherazah, to a rock. He muttered under his breath and kept looking behind him.

"Something tells me you're not crazy about my choice of campsite," I said to him later, as I served him a bowl of my Squire's Stew.

He gave a shudder and pulled his cape around him. "This, my friend," he said, "is an evil place."

"Evil place?" I said.

He nodded. "They call it The Plain of the Dead," he said.

"Interesting name. Let me guess ..." I said, trying not to smile. "Now you're going to tell me why."

2

"The Plain of the Dead," the Peacock said, and his voice trembled. "It is a good name, my friend, trust me."

I nodded, but said nothing.

"It was here," he went on, "that a great battle took place. Many, many years ago," he added, gazing off into the distance. "Before my father's father's father's time ... A mighty battle. A *terrible* battle."

The pair of us were seated on the ground beside the blazing fire. I'd heard tales like this a hundred times before, tales to make the hairs on the back of your neck stand on end and your blood run cold. But that was all they were. Nothing but campfire tales that burned bright in your mind at midnight, but were a harmless heap of ash by dawn.

"On that fateful day," he went on, as his dark eyes glinted in the firelight, "two vast and terrible armies fought to the death on this rocky plain. They stained the ground red with their blood.

"First an army from the East attacked. It was led by a Warrior Lord who held a standard in the shape of a snarling dragon in his hands. The army from the East fell upon the army from the West, which was led by their Golden Empress."

"Sounds nasty," I said.

"As the heaps of the dead grew and grew, the Warrior Lord came face to face with the Golden Empress." The Peacock stared deep into the flames of the fire. "And she trembled at what she saw," he said. "The Warrior Lord's face had been eaten away by the dark arts from which his power came. It was a face of pure evil."

I nodded again. I could tell that this was not the first time the Peacock had told his tale. He knew just when to pause to make his story more dramatic.

"For a moment, the din of the battle stopped," he went on, his voice low and hushed. "But only for a moment. As the sun cast its dying light across the blood-soaked plains, the Warrior Lord swung his curved sword and sliced the Golden Empress's head from her body. 'Victory!' he shouted."

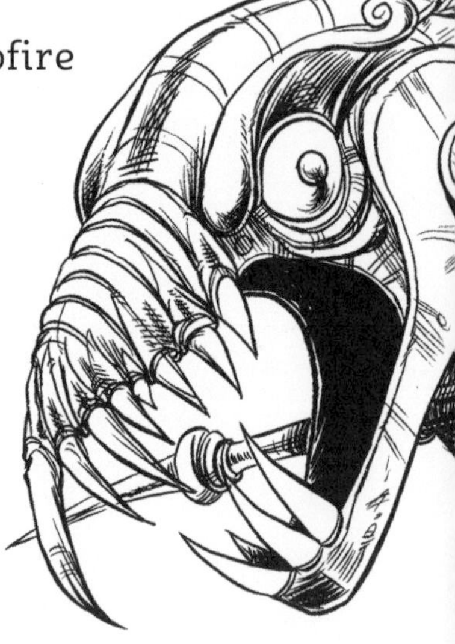

The light from the campfire flames flickered across the merchant's face. I could tell the story wasn't over.

"The next instant, his cry of victory turned to a howl of horror, as he looked down to find the Empress had pushed her dagger deep into his chest. Her dead hand still gripped its handle. As his blood mixed with the blood of the dead, the Warrior Lord shoved his standard into the dusty ground and screamed out with his last breath.

"'I claim this place for the forces of darkness! Evil shall dwell here for ever!'

"And with that he died," the Peacock said, "with the snarling dragon standard looming above his dead body. Ever since that time, this place has indeed been cursed."

I nodded, and put out my hand to throw another piece of wood on the fire. But the merchant stopped me.

"The tale is not yet done," he said, with a tremble in his voice. "It is said that, at the sound of the Warrior Lord's curse, the snarling dragon from the standard sprang to life. It strode over the battlefield and killed all those who were not already dead. Then it feasted on the corpses."

Once again, I nodded, but this time I said nothing. It wouldn't be a campfire tale without a twist in the end – a twist to keep those hairs standing up on the back of the neck. And I didn't have long to wait ...

"What is more, my friend," the merchant said, and his face was deadly serious. "Many believe the dragon still walks these lands ..."

"Uh-huh," I said, as I threw the wood on to the fire and listened to it crackle.

"Indeed," he said. "There are many who say the dragon must always be given fresh meat. They believe that if it gets hungry, it will move away from the battlefield to attack and eat the people of my home town."

"You almost had me worried there," I said, and I gave him a pat on the back. Then I offered him another bowl of stew. "If it weren't for one thing ..."

"What's that?" the Peacock asked, with a wary look in his eye.

"I don't believe in dragons," I said with a laugh.

It was the Peacock's turn to say nothing. He wrapped his cape around him and raised the collar against the chilly wind.

When he spoke, his voice was as cold as the night air itself.

"You should take care, my friend," he said. "Just because you don't believe in something, it doesn't mean it isn't there."

I shrugged. "I'll get back to you on that in the morning," I said.

I stoked up the fire with more wood so that it would last the night. As I did so, a shower of orange sparks flew off into the sky and I saw just how strong the wind had become. All around the plains, a sad and lonely howl rose and fell as it whistled through the rocks and boulders.

It was spooky out there. I might almost have found myself believing in evil warrior lords and snarling dragons. Almost, but not quite.

The mules were all tied up, Jed seemed fine, and I wasn't going to let any spooky stories spoil my night's sleep.

With the fire blazing, hot and bright, I lay down and pulled the blanket over me. I looked around and saw the Peacock doing the same.

I closed my eyes ...

*

The next moment, there was someone beside me shouting my name.

"Wake up, Sir Knight! Wake *up*!"

3

Peacock had worked himself up into a state with his tales of warrior lords and evil dragons. Now, he was dancing round the campfire, hopping from leg to leg. He told me he'd seen a dark shape on the prowl round our camp.

Mind you, dragons or no dragons, something had spooked the mules. They were as jumpy as fleas in a frying-pan, tugging at their ropes and bellowing. And as for Jed, he was rolling his eyes and pawing the ground with his hoofs. Froth bubbled from the corners of his mouth.

"Easy, boy," I said as I stroked his nose and patted his neck. "What is it, Jed? What's spooked you, eh?"

"It's the dragon!" the Peacock hissed. He waved a flaming log from the fire. "Your horse knows it's out there. He can sense it. They all can."

"As I told you," I said, my voice cold, "I don't believe in dragons."

"And as I told you," he snapped back, "just because ..."

"Yes, I know what you said," I broke in.

I pulled a brushwood torch dipped in tar from my belt. Then I lit it from the flaming log that the Peacock had in his hands. I strode out into the darkness.

"You settle those mules," I called back to him. "I'm going to see what's out there."

"Don't be long, Sir Knight," the Peacock babbled. "And please be careful!"

"Yes, yes," I muttered, as I peered into the inky black night.

These merchants, they're all the same. Hard as horseshoe nails when they're after a bargain, but at the first hint of trouble, they go as soft as a princess's feather bed, the lot of them!

Just then, from over to my right, I heard a loud, high scream. I spun round. It was the Peacock. Something had upset him.

"What is it?" I shouted over.

"Sherazah! My mare, Sherazah! She's gone!"

I rushed over to him and gasped. At the end of the row of mules where the white mare had been tied up, there was nothing left but a short bit of rope. It had been snapped and was all frayed.

"Oh, Sherazah, where are you?" the Peacock yelled into the night. His voice was lost in the wind that howled over the empty plain.

He turned to me and the look of panic in his face turned to anger.

"I knew it was a mistake to camp here!" he shouted. "And now my Sherazah has gone! This is all your fault, Sir Knight. You are the bodyguard, you must find her!"

I nodded. I didn't need him to tell me what my job was – not as a bodyguard, or as a knight. With my right hand, I drew my sword. It made a soft, metallic *swoosh*. With my left hand, I lifted up the burning torch. Then, without a word, I plunged into the dark.

"I'll stay here as a look-out," I heard the Peacock call after me.

But a moment later, when I looked back I saw that he had already run to the safety of the campfire. I watched him, a dark shape against the leaping flames. He stoked the fire up – and up and up and up. He wanted it to burn so bright it would frighten off any passing animals – real or not-so-real.

Then I walked on and scanned the dusty ground for hoof-prints. Some way off, I found strange tracks in the dust – I could see that something had been dragged across the ground here. The tracks led towards a rocky crag far ahead.

It wasn't looking good for the Peacock's beloved mare. The animal that had made these tracks was big, and very strong. If it was a wolf, it was the biggest wolf I'd ever come across. Perhaps it was a lion, or some sort of bear? One thing was sure. It wasn't a dragon.

The rocks and boulders came closer. They made strange, jagged shapes. And as I stared, they seemed to turn into terrible monsters with fangs and claws and zigzag crests that ran down their backs ...

I shook my head from side to side. Now I was just being stupid! Next thing you know,

I'd be babbling on about dragons, just like that scaredy-cat Peacock. I went round the rocks. The clouds cleared and the moonlight shone down, clear, bright and silvery white.

And that's when I saw it ... The white horse.

It was slumped next to a rock, in a pool of its own blood. Its neck had been torn open.

I kept the burning torch high above my head as I moved in for a closer look. As I did so, I heard an odd low *hiss* which seemed to come from the shadows to my left. It grew louder for a moment – and then it was gone.

I went closer still. All of a sudden, there was a terrible smell. It wasn't only the poor horse's neck which had been torn open, but also its belly. Its guts had spilled out all over the ground. Whatever had attacked the Peacock's fine white mare had made a stinking mess of it.

But one thing was for sure. This wasn't the work of wolves. I would have heard the yelps and howls of a wolf pack a mile off. No, whatever had dragged the Peacock's horse away to this rocky crag and torn it apart was far more powerful and stealthy than any wolf.

And it also seemed to know just what it was looking for.

I kneeled down and took the ornate gold bridle from the dead horse and slung it over my shoulder. Then I turned on my heels and headed back to the camp. I didn't want to be around when whatever it was came back for a second helping. I found the Peacock packing everything away as fast as he could. He clearly didn't intend to spend the rest of the night in that awful place.

"You read my mind," I said, as I saddled up Jed. "Let's get out of here. If we ride all night, we should make it to town by early morning."

I handed Sherazah's gold bridle to the Peacock.

"There was nothing I could do. Wolves got her," I lied. The last thing I wanted was to spook him even more. "You'll have to ride with me."

We set off straight away. As we galloped across the desolate plain, the mules clopping behind us, the clouds cleared and the full moon shone down. The Peacock leaned forwards in the saddle and hissed in my ear.

"You say wolves got my Sherazah, Sir Knight." He gripped my sleeve tight. "Then, tell me, why can't we hear them howling at the moon?"

4

We galloped all night. Both of us wanted to get as far away as possible from that terrible place. The mules seemed as spooked as we were. A couple of times they tried to break free of their reins and stampede off into the dark.

I whipped them into shape and ignored the Peacock's protests to cut them loose. He was in a panic to get away and not thinking straight. But I knew that he'd thank me for saving his goods in the cold light of morning.

And, trust me, when it came, the light *was* cold.

As we neared the Peacock's home town, pink rays streaked the sky to the east and the birds sang a half-hearted song to welcome the day. But even they seemed unimpressed by their surroundings.

I knew how they felt. The Peacock's home town was a dump.

As we came closer, the Peacock jumped down from Jed and started to pound his fists on the gates of the town – if you could call the rickety group of mud huts a town, that is. Still, to the Peacock, it was home and he seemed glad to be back.

"Open up!" he bellowed. "Open up!" And he hammered on the gates loud enough

to wake a pack of deaf wolfhounds. "Open up, I say!"

All of a sudden, there came the sound of a heavy bolt being pulled back. Then, with a low creak, the gates opened. I peered in. Several burly town guards in tattered chain-mail and dented helmets stood there, wiping the sleep from their eyes.

The Peacock seemed delighted to see them. He collapsed into their arms. He gabbled about being attacked by an evil dragon that had almost eaten him alive. You'd have thought we'd fought off this great fire-breathing dragon with our bare hands. And that the blood-thirsty monster was still hot on our heels, determined to eat every man, woman and child it could sink its drooling fangs into.

But the guards seemed to believe the Peacock's story. The next thing I knew, they were running back down the streets, telling everyone they met what had happened to the merchant out on the plains that night.

The news spread like wildfire. By the time we reached the main square, a welcome committee was waiting for us. The people of the town –

young and old – all clustered round the Peacock and jabbered loudly.

I left them to it. With a mouth more dusty than a monk's sandals, and a thirst to match, I headed for the nearest inn. It was a shabby, rundown little place – just like all the others in this so-called town. But it was open for business, and that was all that mattered.

I pushed open the door and walked in. It was warm and dark inside. When my eyes had got used to the gloom, I strode up to the table in the corner that was the bar, and ordered a tankard of ale. The landlord was a great bear of a man with tangled black hair and one thick

eyebrow. He laughed and pointed up at the goatskin gourds which hung from the hooks above him.

"You're not from round these parts, I take it, Sir Knight," he said. "You'll find no ale here. We have wine or water – and if I were you, I'd stick to the wine. It's cheaper."

"Wine it is," I said. "And make it a large one."

He nodded and produced a flagon the size of a bucket, and then filled it from one of the gourds. "Have this one for free," he said as he handed me the flagon. "You look as if you need it after the night you've had."

Like I said, news travelled fast in this town.

I thanked him, put the flagon to my lips and took a long drink. The golden wine lit a fire from my neck to my belly. It had the kick of a mule and the taste of wet goat. But it washed away the dust in my mouth, so I didn't complain.

I took the flagon with me, as I crossed the warm, dark room to a rough, low table in the corner. I sat down and stretched out my legs. It had been a long, hard night and a long, hard two weeks on the road. I was worn out. Now at last, I could put my feet up and relax. I took another swig from the flagon and sat back in my chair with a long sigh of happiness.

I should have known better.

Just at that moment, what looked like a heap of dusty rags in the corner opposite me let out a loud burp. I turned and saw a wrinkly old man with a yellowish face. His hair was thin and his clothes were tatty. Dark, shifty eyes peered out from under hooded eyelids. He clambered to his feet and shuffled over.

I groaned. The last thing I wanted right now was company.

"Good morning, Sir Knight," he said in a whiny voice. "I don't suppose you'd buy a little wine for a poor merchant down on his luck."

I looked over at the landlord.

"Pour him a drink," I said.

The landlord tutted, but poured out a flagon of wine all the same.

"Thank you, Sir Knight," the old merchant said. He grabbed the flagon and gulped back the wine. Then he wiped his mouth with a grimy hand and gave me a smile that showed his rotten teeth. "Of course," he said as he settled down beside me, "I wasn't always the poor old man you see before you." He turned his weasel face towards me.

'Here we go,' I thought, another sob-story of lost hopes and shattered dreams. I'd heard them all in my time. Sure enough, on his second flagon, the tatty old merchant really got going.

He told me how he'd once been the richest merchant in town. But then the big-city merchants tricked him, robbers stole his mules and the evil dragon out there on the plains ruined trade for everyone.

"There's a curse on this town," he said, as he slurped his wine. "Take my advice, Sir Knight, and get out while you still can. *I* would if I had any money."

"Not before I pick up my pay," I said. I pushed back my chair and stood up.

I was about to leave, when the door flew open and in stepped a young woman. Even in the gloom of the inn, I could tell she was beautiful. Her hair was as black as ebony and her eyes were sapphire blue. Her clothes were as tattered and torn as the old merchant's, but she was as dazzling as any princess.

Our eyes met and the strangest thing happened. My heart beat faster than a squire's at his first tournament. My mouth became as dry as dust again. The same thing must have happened to her, because she stared back at me, a look of surprise on her beautiful face.

'This is what happens when you drink the local wine,' I thought, as I tried to stay cool and collected. For a moment, I thought the Ragged Beauty was going to speak to me. Instead, she turned to the old Heap-of-Rags at the table.

“Father!” she cried. “When you didn’t come home last night, I was frantic with worry …” She rushed over to him. “Still, no harm done,” she added. “So long as you’re safe.”

The old man grunted and pushed her away.

“I’ve made you some breakfast with the last of the eggs,” the Ragged Beauty went on. She smiled. “Why don’t you come home with me now, before it gets cold.”

The old man scowled. “Why can’t you just leave me alone!” he protested, as he got to his feet. “Can’t a man have some peace and quiet without being pestered by his good-for-nothing daughter?”

I expected the Ragged Beauty to react to this, but instead she wiped a tear from her eye and turned away.

“I’m sorry I’m such a disappointment to you, Father,” she said in a low voice.

“Oh, stop your snivelling and take me home!” the ungrateful old man snarled. “Or my eggs will be ruined.”

I wanted to box the old brute’s ears for him, but I knew that would only upset his lovely daughter. So I stepped aside as they left, and waited for my head to clear and my heartbeat to return to normal.

I had to find the Peacock and sort out the little matter of my fifty gold coins. I was just about to leave when who should walk in, but the Peacock himself.

"Ah, Sir Knight," he said. "Just the person I was looking for."

"Same here," I said. We stepped out into the bright sun of the town square.

"We had a lucky escape last night," the Peacock said. "Despite your foolish decision to sleep out on the plains, even after my warnings ..."

I said nothing. He could save his stories of the dragons and battles of years past for people who liked that sort of thing.

"Still," he went on, "the mules all made it here safe and sound, and my goods are safe too. A job well done, Sir Knight. I am very

pleased." He pulled a bag of gold coins from inside his robes and handed it over. "I have, of course, had to keep a coin or two to cover the loss of my horse, Sherazah ..."

I opened the purse and tipped the gold coins into my hand. There were ten missing.

'No surprise there,' I thought, as I put them back in the purse. They're all the same, these merchants ...

"She was a very costly horse, Sir Knight, as I'm sure you'll understand."

It was clear there was no point arguing with him. I smiled. Forty gold

coins was still a tidy sum. And not bad for a fortnight's work, I told myself. Not bad at all. It was the most money I'd had in my hand for a long time.

But when I looked up, I saw we were being watched. On the opposite side of the square, hanging about in the shade, were two mean-looking men with rusty armour and cheap swords. One of them had a dented helmet on his head, like a witch's cauldron. The other, I saw when he smiled back at me, had wonky brown teeth.

They were swords-for-hire, down on their luck. I knew their sort, of course. They would have arrived in town on a job like mine, then stayed around

to spend their money and get into trouble. One thing you could bet on in a little town like this, was that there would always be trouble. And it usually started with a pretty face in an inn ...

I thought of the Ragged Beauty and made up my mind that I wouldn't get drawn into any adventures because of her. Just as soon as I'd had a little bit of sleep, I was going to get out of this fly-blown town, fast – Ragged Beauty or no Ragged Beauty.

*

I took a room above the inn. The landlord promised me that his beds were the biggest, softest ones in town. After I'd put Jed in the stables round the back, I took him up on the offer.

He wasn't wrong about the beds.

I closed the shutters to cut out the glare of the morning sun. Then I kicked off my boots and fell onto the bed. After two weeks of sleeping out on the hard earth of the plain, the bed felt as soft as a snowdrift lined with feathers. I was asleep before my head hit the pillow.

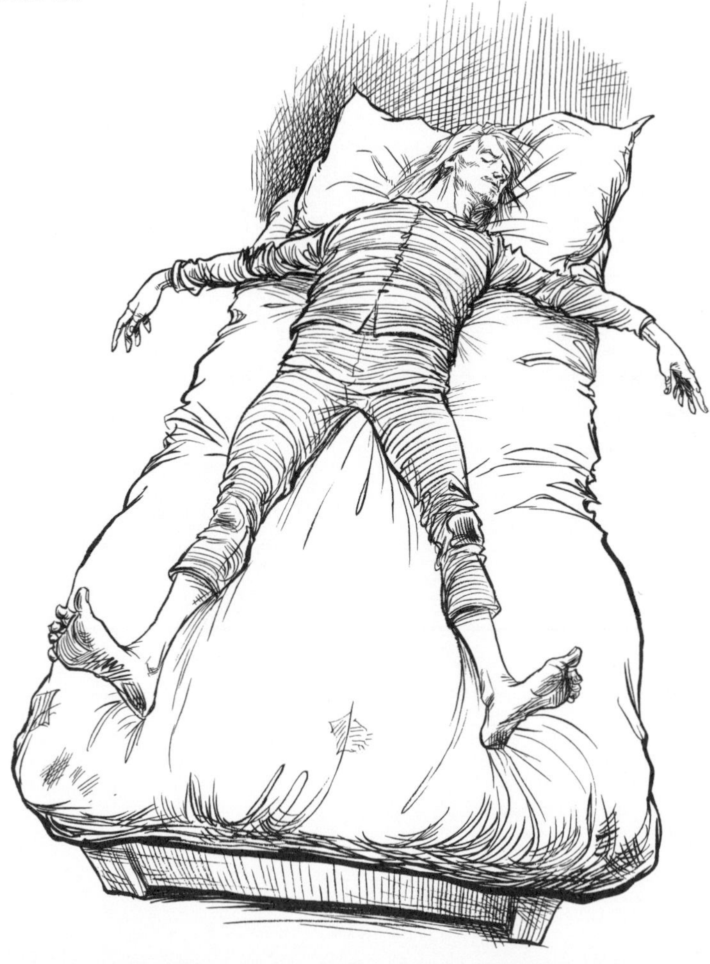

The next thing I knew, a blare of loud music woke me up. I could hear the blast of horns, the beat of drums, the clash of cymbals. And on top of it all was the sound of excited voices.

I climbed out of bed, went to the window and opened the shutters. The sun was low and orange. I must have been asleep all day.

Down below, the square was full of townsfolk, as they jostled and clamoured and craned their necks to see the parade that was slowly making its way along the main street. It was *wild*, I can tell you.

I spotted a few of the people I'd seen that morning. It never takes me long to get to know a new place. There were two of the city-guards. A bunch of shifty, travelling knights. And there was the Peacock.

I frowned. He seemed to be talking to ...

But no, it couldn't be. I looked more closely. And yes, indeed. He was deep in conversation with old Heap-of-Rags.

'How odd,' I thought.

What happened next was even odder. I saw the Peacock slip the old merchant a small bag.

Old Heap-of-Rags scuttled away, the bag of money clutched in his thin hands. I knew he could only be headed for one place – the inn, and for as much wine as he could guzzle.

'But why,' I wondered, 'had the Peacock been so generous?'

He had taken coins from my wages for his horse. So I knew he didn't give his money away for nothing.

I looked back at the parade itself. Half the people of the town had turned out to watch it, and they were all pushing forwards to the beat of the drums and the clash of the cymbals. It was quite a party – if that was what it was.

There were musicians and dancers, jugglers and stilt-walkers, as well as the hundreds of rowdy townsfolk keeping in step with them. I looked back along the line of party goers as it made its way along the

streets of the town. And then, coming round a corner, I saw four big burly men dressed in black.

Lifted up on their shoulders was a huge gold throne set on two long poles. A princess, or maybe even a queen, sat upright and still as the throne swayed above the heads of the crowd. She was wearing purple robes that shimmered in the sun, a silver turban and a silver veil which hung down over her face. There were necklaces around her neck, bangles at her wrists and ankles, and rings on every finger. And every necklace, bangle and ring was studded with bright jewels that sparkled in the low sun.

As she passed under my window, I gazed into the princess's eyes. I knew who she was at once. Those large, clear eyes, as blue as sparkling sapphires. She was the Ragged Beauty – but no longer ragged, for now she was dressed up in all the finery of a real princess.

But something was wrong. I could tell that from the instant our eyes met.

There, plain to see in those beautiful blue eyes, was sheer, numb panic.

“Help me!” her eyes seemed to cry out to me. “Sweet Sir Knight, please help me!”

5

With no time to think, I grabbed my sword and was down the stairs of the inn before the clash of the last cymbal had died away. I was running for the door when something caught my eye.

There, in the shadows at the back of the inn, sat old Heap-of-Rags. He had yet another flagon of wine raised to his lips. A wave of rage swept through me.

“Your daughter,” I cried out. “Where are they taking her?”

“It’s none of your business,” he slurred. “She’s gone for the good of the town ...”

"Gone where?" I said.

"... For the good of the town ..."

"What do you mean?" I shouted. I grabbed his dirty robes. "What are they going to do to her?"

"Good of the town," he said again, and I saw that his bloodshot eyes were out of focus. "It's better this way ... I've got money now ... To leave this town ... Start again ..."

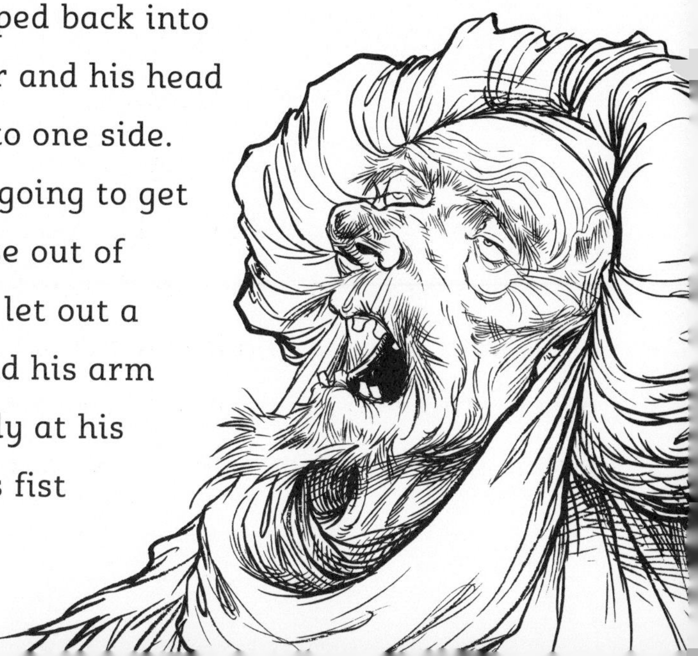

I stared back at the old man for a moment. My lip curled with disgust, then I let him go. He slumped back into the chair and his head flopped to one side. I wasn't going to get any sense out of him. He let out a snore and his arm fell limply at his side. His fist opened and the Peacock's silver coins dropped to the floor.

'That's how much his daughter means to him,' I thought. I turned away and strode to the door.

I understood now. Peacock and the townsfolk had decided to have a little party, with the Ragged Beauty as guest of honour – and paid her awful old father for her. It was clear from the look in her eyes that she wasn't too thrilled – and that's where I came in. Like I said before, in small towns like this, trouble is always just around the corner, and it looked like I'd run into a whole heap of it.

At the stables, I found Jed had been fed, watered and brushed down – but the stable-boy who had looked after him was nowhere to be seen. I left some copper coins for him, and a couple more for the brushwood torches I took from a shelf. It was getting dark and I didn't want to be stuck out there on the plains without a torch for light.

I put Jed's saddle on, jumped onto his back and spurred him on. We rode along the empty streets fast. Then, as I steered us out of the

town gates, I saw the lights of the parade twinkling far ahead. It was making its way along the rocky path towards the barren plain.

'What can I, just one knight, do against a whole town?' I thought bitterly.

Even so, I followed them, taking care to stay so far back that no one would see me. Then, as they set off across the plain, I skirted round to the east. I kept myself hidden behind rocks and boulders, and stayed upwind so that

no one could hear the beat of Jed's hoofs on the dusty ground – not that they were likely to hear anything above the racket they were still making.

An hour or so later, I saw the parade come to a halt. I got down off Jed, tied him up and crept closer for a better look. I promised myself that I'd take on the whole town if a single hair on the Ragged Beauty's head had been harmed. I silently drew my sword and prayed that I wouldn't have to.

As the pipes and trumpets blasted and the drums and cymbals clashed, the four hefty men carrying the throne put down their load. Then one of them stepped forwards and cut the ropes which, I now saw, had tied the Ragged Beauty to the gold chair. They pulled her roughly to her feet.

Anger rose up in me as they bundled her across to a tall narrow rock, where they tied her up, with her back to the rock. I went closer, my knuckles white as I gripped my sword.

This was it. They weren't expecting me, so I had surprise on my side. I could take out two guards with one blow of my sword, fell the 3rd with another blow, and drop the 4th with a throw of my dagger. That just left the rest of the town to tear me limb from limb for spoiling their party. Still, if I could free the Ragged Beauty and give her time to escape while I went down in a fight with the townsfolk, then it would be worth it.

I had tensed every muscle in my body and was about to leap out, when the oddest thing happened.

The music suddenly stopped, the voices fell quiet and the crowd turned on their heels. Only the Ragged Beauty was left – slumped and unable to move. Her body shook with sobs, as the entire parade set off across the plain, back the way they had come.

I could tell that the townsfolk were ashamed, embarrassed. Some of them stared down at their feet as they shuffled away. Yet none of them looked back. They had left her there, all alone, tied to a rock on the barren plain.

I waited until the coast was clear, then I stepped forward. As I came close, the Ragged Beauty looked up, her eyes wide with surprise above the silver veil. I pulled it back, and saw an ugly gag over her beautiful mouth.

That's not all I saw. Up close, the clothes she had been dressed up in were cheap and tatty.

The jewels she wore were nothing but brass and glass, cheap trinkets the lot of them.

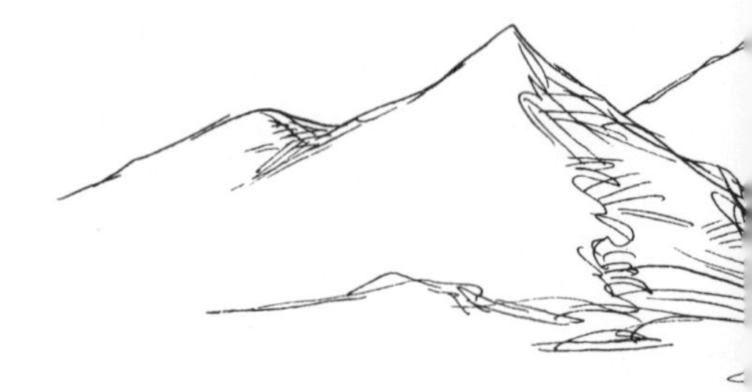

What was going on? There was only one person who could tell me and that was the Ragged Beauty herself. I put my hand out to remove the gag when a gruff voice rang out behind me.

"Oi!" it bellowed. "Not so fast!"

6

I spun round to see two low-life knights behind me. I knew who they were at once. It was Cauldron Head and Wonky Tooth, my old chums from the market square. The two with their rusty armour, cheap swords and mean sneers.

They must have tracked me across the rocky plains. I cursed myself. I'd been careless, terribly careless. I'd been so intent on keeping track of the parade and what to do when I caught up with it, I'd failed to notice that I was being tracked myself. Now I'd have to pay for being so careless.

"Well, well, and what've we got here?" said Wonky Tooth, with his crooked grin. "Quite the knight in shining armour, ain't we?" he sneered.

"Yeah," his friend Cauldron Head said with a leer. "About to rescue a fair damsel in distress ... What a noble deed. We're impressed, Sir Knight."

I said nothing. If these two rascals had ever done a single knightly deed in their lives, then I'd snap my lance for firewood. They were squires gone to the bad, most like. Good-for-nothing robbery and moonlight ambushes were more their line of work.

Still, they were armed and dangerous.

Wonky Tooth drew an evil, curved sword, which he waved at me. It had flecks of rust along the blade, but still it looked as if it could do me real harm.

"Stand away from the lady," he cried, "and hand over the purse we saw that stuck-up merchant give you."

"Yeah, hand it over, and we'll make it nice and quick," Cauldron Head added, as he drew a menacing finger across his throat. He pulled out a great two-handed broadsword, and gave me an evil grin. "Who knows?" he said. "We might even let the lady go."

"Nice offer, Fatso," I said as I drew my own sword. I smiled. "I'm sorry but if you want my money, you're going to have to work a bit harder to get it, you over-fed bully.

And, by the way, what *is* that on your head? Looks like a potty ..."

I saw a change come over Cauldron Head's face. He was getting a bit steamed up. Amazing what an insult or two can do.

"This one's mine," he snapped at Wonky Tooth. "Stand aside. I'll take care of him."

Then, with a bellow like an angry bull, he lowered his head and charged at me. The great broadsword whistled through the air as he swung it above his head.

I let him get close to me – closer than that fool had any right to get – before I stepped nimbly to one side. I deflected his heavy blow with a low counter-thrust of my own. Our swords clashed so hard that judders of pain shot up my body from my hand to my neck.

Cauldron Head roared with fury. The great oaf had the power of an ox, but he was heavy and clumsy, and slow on his feet.

I darted to the left and lunged as Cauldron Head turned back to face me, slashing up and across with my sword. The tip of my blade made contact. In an instant, it traced an angry red line, dotted with blood, right the way across his cheek – and made his bellows all the louder.

With a howl of animal rage, he lifted his broadsword and swung it down with all his force. At that very moment, Wonky Tooth stuck out a crafty leg and sent me flying. I expect he was trying to do his friend a favour. Instead, he saved my life.

Cauldron Head's great broadsword – which would have split me in two from head to foot – crashed down on a rock to my left. He had to let it go and I knew this was my chance. I twisted round and threw my own sword, like a dagger, direct at Wonky Tooth's neck.

The razor-sharp blade flashed in the moonlight as it flew through the air in a smooth arc. Wonky Tooth never stood a chance. It cut through his leather breastplate like a hot knife through butter and plunged deep into the base of his neck.

I reached out, grasped Cauldron Head's broadsword from the dust and got to my feet to face him. A look of dismay flashed across his face as he turned to look first at his friend, then at me.

"It's just you and me now, Potty Hat." I smiled.

With a roar like a wounded bear, Cauldron Head pulled the knife from his belt and threw himself at me.

In a flash, I dropped to my knees. I lowered my body and gripped the broadsword tight.

Cauldron Head couldn't stop himself. The next instant, there was a loud *crunch* and an awful *squelch* as the great clumsy oaf fell on to the blade and spiked himself on it. My shoulders jarred as they absorbed the shock.

I looked up. Cauldron Head's face was inches from my own, a look of stupid surprise carved into his ugly features.

"*Urrgghh*!" He gave a soft groan as his eyes glazed over and drool flecked with blood dribbled down from his mouth.

With a grunt of effort, I pushed him aside. He slumped to the ground, his dead hands gripping the sword fixed in his chest.

I climbed to my feet, weary. It was just as I had thought. These two weren't knights. They had no fighting skills learned on the tournament field or in dangerous quests. No, they were just a couple of jumped-up squires who had skipped sword practice once too often – and now they'd paid the price.

Still, it was a high price to pay, and I felt bad about what I'd had to do to them. It could be a dirty business being a free lance knight.

"*Wffll mmffllmm!*"

I turned round.

The Ragged Beauty was still tied to the rock in her satin robe and cheap trinkets. I walked over to her, untied her and took the gag from her mouth.

What with her heart-breaking sobs, it was a few moments before she could get her breath. When she did, her sapphire blue eyes flashed as they looked into mine.

"You're safe now," I told her.

"But, Sir Knight," she gasped. And her voice trembled with feeling. "I'm not. And neither are you ..."

7

"What do you mean?" I asked the Ragged Beauty.

"We're both in terrible danger," she cried, her face twisted with fear. "We must leave this evil place at once!" She swallowed hard, and tears welled in her eyes. "At once, Sir Knight! Do you hear me?"

I heard her loud and clear, but it made no sense.

"If you're worried about the townsfolk, you don't need to be," I promised her. "They won't be back anytime soon."

"It's not them," she sobbed. "It's this place. We must leave ..."

"All right, all right," I said to calm her. She'd had a bad shock, I could see that. I'd have to go along with her fears, even if they were silly. "But where do you want to go?" I asked. "Not back to the town ..."

"No," she said, her voice little more than a whisper. "No, I can't go back there. Not

now ..." She fell to her knees, as the tears streamed down her cheeks. "Not after what they did to me ..."

I pulled a hanky from my pocket and held it out to her. She took it and dabbed it to her cheeks.

"They chose me as the sacrifice," she sobbed, and her words cut the night air like a blade. "I begged my father not to, but ... but ... Oh, Sir Knight, he was only interested in the money ..."

"Much good may it do him," I growled. Old Heap-of-Rags would have spent it all in the inn by now.

"They always choose the poor ones," the Ragged Beauty went on. "It's never the rich merchants who offer up their daughters. And now ..." She shook her head. "I can never go back. Ever. If I did, they'd know that there was no

sacrifice made to the dragon, and then ...
Oh, Sir Knight, I have nowhere else to go."

As she spoke, everything fell into place. The Peacock's wild story, the townsfolk hanging on his every word, and then the wild parade out on to this barren plain.

Of course! They really believed that if they tied this poor girl to a rock and left her out here, then this dragon of theirs would leave them alone. If it wasn't so evil, I would have had a good laugh at them all.

I smiled at the Ragged Beauty in her fake jewels. Maybe the townsfolk also thought the brass trinkets and glass beads would attract this dragon, just as they do in all the best campfire tales.

"Don't worry," I said, as she wiped the tears from her sapphire blue eyes. "I've seen my fair share of crazy things as a free lance, from creepy hags to evil witches. If there were such things as dragons, then I would have met a few in my travels, trust me." I laughed. "Relax, Blue Eyes," I said. "This dragon of yours doesn't exist."

"If it ... d ... doesn't, th ... th ... then ..." she stammered, her eyes wide with fear as she stared past me. "Wh ... wh ... what is *that*?"

At that moment, an awful stink filled the air, a mix of bad eggs and rotten flesh. And from just behind me came a soft, wheezing hiss ...

'No,' I thought, 'it couldn't be ... Could it?'

There was only one way to find out. I gripped the handle of my sword as hard as I could, and I slowly turned around ...

And wished that I hadn't. For there, in front of me, was the most vile monster I had ever seen.

It had a long, knobbly body, four powerful legs, and brutal talons. Two evil, bloodshot eyes stared out from its scaly face. And when it opened its huge fang-filled jaws, the shocking stink of decay became a hundred times stronger.

"*Kkhhhhhhhsss!*"

It let out a low, wheezing hiss. A grey forked tongue flicked in and out, in and out from between its dripping, yellow fangs, tasting the air. Its unblinking eyes stared past me. I realised with a jolt that the monster had its gaze fixed on the Ragged Beauty.

Or rather, on the Ragged Beauty's neck.

She was frozen to the spot with fear, unable to move a muscle. I had to think fast.

"Your necklace," I whispered to her.

"My n … n … necklace?" she whispered back.

"Yes," I told her. "Give it to me now."

She tore the big chain of sparkly glass jewels from her neck and held it out. I grabbed it, and waved it in front of the dragon's face.

"Here you are, you great smelly monster!" I said in my sweetest, softest voice.

"You like these, don't you?" I went on as I backed away. "Come on then. What are you waiting for?"

The dragon swayed. Its bloodshot eyes looked from the necklace to the Ragged

Beauty, and back again. It was as if it was trying to choose between her white flesh and the sparkly bits of glass in my hand. Its tongue flicked the air. Its talons scratched at the dusty ground.

Then, with a wheeze and a roar, it flung back its head, swung round and lumbered towards me.

I backed off as fast as I could, trying to draw the monster as far away from the Ragged Beauty as possible. And that's when it happened ...

I tripped over the dead body of Cauldron Head and went sprawling to the ground. I landed hard, the breath was knocked out of me and I dropped my sword.

The monster saw its chance. With a booming roar, it jumped at me and grabbed my left arm – the one holding the necklace – in its massive jaws. If it hadn't been for my armour, it would have bitten clean through my arm right then and there. As it was, I was held fast by the monster's strong grip.

The dragon was so desperate to get hold of the sparkly necklace that it began to shake its massive head from side to side, and I was tossed about like a rag doll.

The last thing I remember was my face hurtling towards a huge rock that stood out from the barren ground.

Then blackness ...

*

When I came to, I found that the monster was dragging me across the rocky ground, with my arm still clutched in its jaws, like a hungry castle dog with a bone. There was only one thing for it.

I did what I always do at hopeless times like this.

I played dead.

In the dust and the dark ahead, I could make out a small opening in the rocky landscape. The monster was heading for it. It lumbered through the narrow crack – I was knocked against the sides of the wall as it did so – and then down into its den. The smell was foul.

There, it began to shake me around again until the necklace fell from the grasp of my cold "dead" hands.

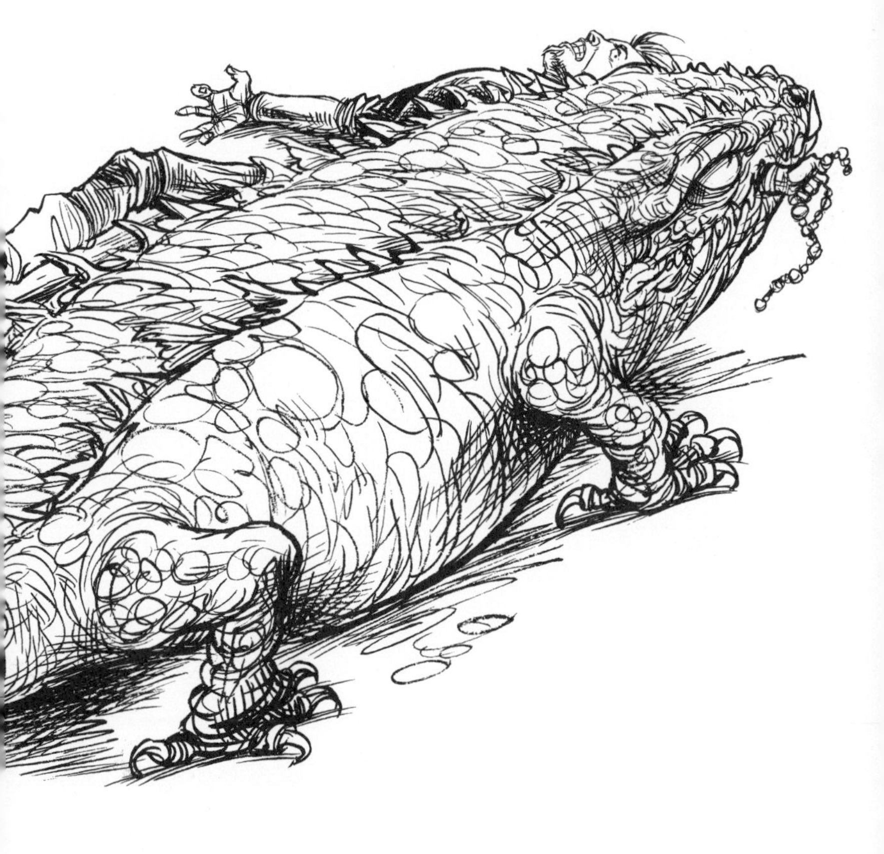

Satisfied for a moment, the monster spat me out. I rolled into the corner and played dead for all I was worth. The disgusting dragon snuffled and drooled over the glass trinket.

I opened one eye. A beam of moonlight cut down from above into the dragon's terrible den.

In the gloom, I saw the monster toss the necklace to one side with its nose, and turn to me with an evil hiss. I let out a groan of despair. It had had the starter, now it wanted the main course. That was me – and, without my sword, I knew there was nothing I could do to protect myself.

'So this is it,' I thought. This was how I was to meet my end, as a feast for a dragon.

And I had thought it was just a local fairy tale! I should have paid more attention to the Peacock's words at the campfire. There's always *some* truth in that kind of story.

Of course, it was the word "dragon" that was to blame. To me, dragons only live in fairy stories, where they have wings and forked tails and breath of fire. They weren't real. Not like the monster that loomed up before me now. But I had to admit, as it opened its massive jaws, "dragon" seemed as good a name as any for the ugly monster. And as for its breath ...

I got to my feet and clenched my fists. If I was about to be eaten alive, then I'd do my very best to stick in the monster's throat. With a stinking roar of anger, the dragon started to lumber towards me.

8

Then all of a sudden, the beam of moonlight that had shone into the dragon's den was blocked out.

"Sir Knight! Sir Knight!" someone called from above.

It was the Ragged Beauty.

The monster stopped for a moment at the sound of her voice.

"Quick, take this!" she shouted, and the next moment I heard something clatter down and land at my side. I put out my hand and it closed round the handle of my sword. And not a moment too soon! The monster came at me again, its jaws so wide that I could see what was left of its last feast stuck in its teeth.

"Eat this, dragon breath!" I roared, as I thrust my sword deep into the monster's open mouth. There was a *grind* and a *crunch* and a *squelch* as I drove the blade deeper. The blade went into its gullet, its gizzard and down its gaping throat until, with my arm stuck deep into the monster, I stabbed its black heart.

A rush of blood and bile soaked me, and the stink almost overpowered me. I gagged for breath, then I pulled my sword back out of the great, dying monster as it sank to the floor of its den. Soon it lay still, its great body lifeless at last.

I looked up to see the Ragged Beauty climb down into the cave to join me.

“Oh, Sir Knight,” she cried. “I can’t tell you how grateful I am.”

‘You could try,’ I thought.

“I’m for ever in your debt, Sir Knight. Tell me how I can repay you and I shall do so, I promise ...”

This was more like it. “Oh, it was nothing,” I said. “All in a day’s work for a free lance.”

I pulled one of the torches from my belt. “Now let’s throw some light on the matter,” I said.

I struck my flints, and the sparks lit the dry torch, which crackled into flames. The firelight lit up the dark cave.

The Ragged Beauty gasped. I didn't blame her. All around us was a picture of sheer horror. It was like a nightmare. The dead monster itself was sprawled out over the floor, its blood and bile soaking into the dust. Now I

could see it close up, the dragon looked much older. Lines and bumps and jagged scars decorated its foul body.

'Just how long has this terrible beast lurked here?' I asked myself.

The answer lay all about me, in the bones of its countless victims – victims that must have stretched back hundreds and hundreds of years. I staggered back, crunching on the old bones under my feet.

Large bones, small bones. Leg bones, thumb bones, hip and finger bones – some separated, some still connected. Ribs and spines, and papery skulls, their empty yellow eye-sockets staring back at me. It was as if I'd fallen down into a tomb that everyone else had forgotten about long ago.

And there, amid these gruesome piles of bones, were the tatty glass trinkets that the dragon's victims had worn as they went to their deaths.

"Come, Sir Knight," the Ragged Beauty said. "Let us leave this terrible place."

I nodded and was about to follow her, when something caught my eye. I took the Ragged Beauty's hand and the two of us walked deeper into the dragon's den.

I raised my torch up high. And to my surprise, there among the oldest of the dragon's victims, was a treasure trove beyond my wildest dreams. It glittered and gleamed in the light of my torch.

There were sword belts full of jewels, gold breastplates, silver charms and helmets of finest gold, studded with gems and jewels …

And at the centre, sticking up from the pile of priceless items, was one item more amazing than all the rest.

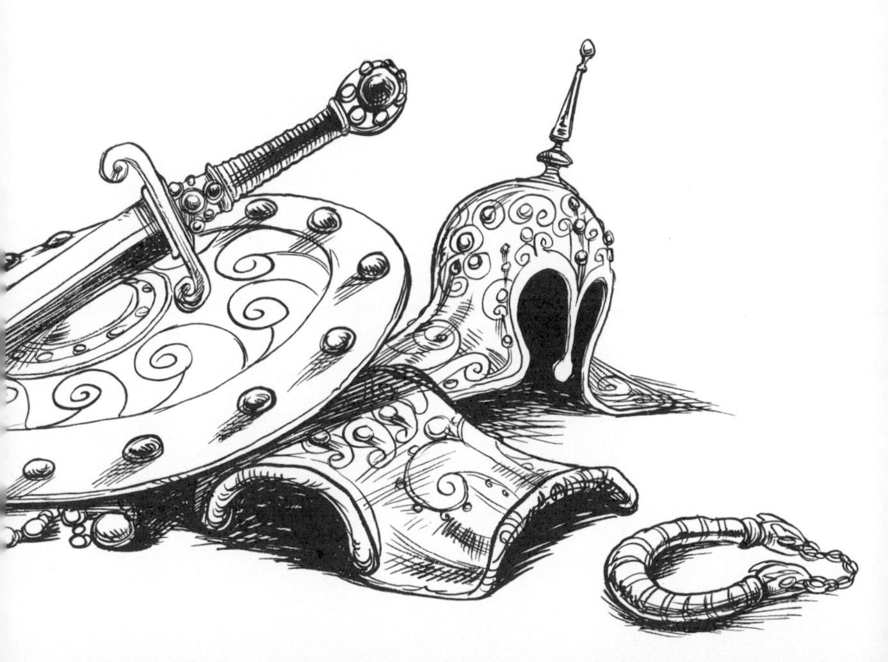

It was a gold standard, adorned with jewels. At one end it had a snarling dragon – and at the other was a skeleton hand still holding it, the bone split at the elbow. Close by was a broken rib-cage with a golden dagger stuck between the curved bones.

The Peacock's story came flooding back to me. It was true, all of it. I had scoffed at it, and yet here was proof of that mighty battle all around us. Beside me, I could feel the Ragged Beauty tremble.

"Please, please, Sir Knight," she said, her voice low and full of fear. "I cannot bear to stay in this terrible place a moment longer."

She had a point. The whole place reeked of death and decay. But before we left it far behind us, like a bad dream after a campfire tale, there was one last thing I had to do.

*

As the sun rose on a bright new day, I spurred Jed on. He trotted faster and, for a moment, the rein between us and the two scruffy horses that had belonged to Wonky Tooth and Cauldron Head went tight.

I turned to check that the precious loads on their backs were still in place. And, as I did so, my cheek brushed against the beautiful dark hair of the Ragged Beauty, who was behind me in the saddle, her arms around my waist. She had been fast asleep for the last hour, but there was a little smile playing on her lips.

It had taken me three or four trips down into the dark den to gather up every bit of the

dragon's hoard. Now it clinked and clunked on the backs of the two scruffy horses behind me.

As we rode north, away from that cursed plain, I tried to picture the battles from all those years ago. A vile lizard, which feasted on the dead, had been attracted by the smell of death as it drifted on the cold wind. The lizard had waddled across the rocky plain from some far-off swamp or muddy river. It must have been amazed when it got to that blood-soaked battlefield.

All those dead bodies. All those sparkly jewels. No wonder the lizard had found a cosy cave close by where it could drag the dead bodies and eat their flesh in peace. And, as the bones had piled up, so had the gold and the jewels, and the lizard had grown to the size of a monster.

That was how the story had started. And so, shepherds and merchants stumbled back to the town to tell their stories of the dragon they had seen.

Of course, when the monster had eaten all the dead bodies from the battle, it had needed to become more and more bold. It hadn't wanted to abandon its glittering hoard of treasure, and so it had stayed in its den. Only these days, it came out to attack people sleeping around campfires, rather than the bodies of the dead. Over the years, the townsfolk had learned that they had to keep feeding it if they wanted to stay safe. And so they chose people to sacrifice to the monster for its food.

They chose the poor, the weak and the helpless ... Isn't that always the way?

I felt the Ragged Beauty shift in the saddle behind me.

She was safe now, and the Peacock and the townsfolk would understand, after a year or two, that they were safe too. Not that we cared. No, we were leaving it all behind us.

I smiled. I had enough gold to set myself up in a fine castle as a lord, and the Ragged Beauty had agreed to become my lady.

And as for Wormrick, he would become a fine knight. With my new wealth, I'd make sure of that. Not for him the life of a free lance with all its dangers.

No, when Wormrick had earned his spurs, he would become a bonded knight. He would serve a rich lord, who would take pride in his successes and respect his fine deeds.

And who would be that rich lord? Why, none other than yours truly – me!

Don't get me wrong. I'd loved the life of a free lance, but neither Jed nor I was getting any younger. Now I was rich beyond my wildest dreams and, more precious by far, I had the love of a fine woman. As I rode towards the rising sun, I knew that my free lance days were behind me for ever.

It had been a good life, but the best was still to come.

Our books are tested
for children and young people by
children and young people.

Thanks to everyone who consulted on
a manuscript for their time and effort in
helping us to make our books better
for our readers.